# JACOB'S
## Room to Choose

**Sarah** and **Ian Hoffman**
Illustrated by **Chris Case**

**Magination Press • Washington, DC**
**American Psychological Association**

For Aubrie Reeves, who taught us that education really does work. And for Sam and Ruby, in every way and always—*SH & IH*

For Olivia—*CC*

**Magination Press**
Books for Kids From the
American Psychological Association

Order books at maginationpress.org or call 1-800-374-2721.

Book design by Gwen Grafft
Printed by Phoenix Color, Hagerstown, MD

Library of Congress Cataloging-in-Publication Data

Names: Hoffman, Sarah, author. | Hoffman, Ian, 1962- author. |
 Case, Chris, 1976- illustrator.
Title: Jacob's room to choose / by Sarah and Ian Hoffman ;
 illustrated by Chris Case.
Description: Washington, DC : Magination Press, [2019] | "American
 Psychological Association." | Summary: After Jacob and Sophie are
 prevented from using their school's bathrooms, their teacher helps her
 students write new rules about who can use which bathroom.
Identifiers: LCCN 2018046751| ISBN 9781433830730 (hardcover) |
 ISBN 1433830736 (hardcover)
Subjects: | CYAC: Gender identity—Fiction. | Bathrooms—Fiction. |
 Schools—Fiction.
Classification: LCC PZ7.H67516 Jam 2019 | DDC [E]—dc23 LC
record available at https://lccn.loc.gov/2018046751

Manufactured in the United States of America
10 9 8 7 6 5 4 3 2 1

The carpet was warm. The bunnies were funny.
Jacob and Sophie loved library time.

"Okay, kids," said Ms. Reeves. "We've got 10 minutes left.
Does anyone need to use the bathroom before we head back to class?"

Jacob and Sophie raised their hands.

They stopped outside the bathroom doors.
"Do you think it's OK?" asked Sophie.
"I don't know," said Jacob.

Sophie walked through one door.
Jacob took a deep breath and walked through the other.

Two boys were at the sinks.
They stared at Jacob standing in the doorway.
Jacob knew what that look meant.
He turned and ran out.

Jacob stood in the hall, his heart pounding.
Just then Sophie ran out of her bathroom.
It was hard for Jacob to talk.
"Did you get chased out?"
Sophie nodded.

Back at the library, Sophie shifted from foot to foot.
"I need to use the bathroom," she said.
Ms. Reeves was confused.
"Didn't you and Jacob just go to the bathroom?"

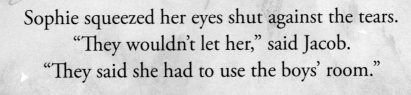

Sophie squeezed her eyes shut against the tears.
"They wouldn't let her," said Jacob.
"They said she had to use the boys' room."

Ms. Reeves looked inside the bathroom. It was empty.
"Anybody in there?"
There was no response.
She waited in the hall while Sophie and Jacob went in.

"Better?" asked Ms. Reeves.
"Yes," said Sophie.
"Has this happened before?"
Sophie and Jacob glanced at each other.

"Usually I don't go at school," said Jacob.
Sophie started to cry again. "It's not fair," said Sophie.
"No," agreed Ms. Reeves. She gave them both a hug. "It isn't."

Back in the classroom,
Ms. Reeves drew on the board.
"What do these pictures mean?"
"Boys and girls!" the kids shouted happily.

"OK," said Ms. Reeves,
"but how do you know?"
"The girl has long hair," said Emily,
"and she's wearing a dress."
"The boy is wearing shorts," said Noah.
"And a t-shirt."

"Now I want each of you to stand near the picture that looks like you," said Ms. Reeves.

Jacob and Sophie looked at Ms. Reeves. Ms. Reeves winked back.

"Hold on," called Ms. Reeves. "Noah, you have long hair. That sign shows short hair. And Emily, you're wearing pants, but the person on that sign is wearing a dress."

Ms. Reeves scratched her head. "Why don't you switch places?"
Noah shrugged and walked to where Ms. Reeves pointed.

Emily looked at the group of boys.
"I don't want to stand there," she said.
"Why not?" asked Ms. Reeves.
"Because I'm a girl."

Ms. Reeves studied the kids again. "You know what? A lot of you don't look like the signs. Let's try this: look at the person next to you and help them stand next to people who look like them."

Arguing and giggling, the kids shuffled and reshuffled until everyone found a place to stand.

Ms. Reeves pointed at the board.
"Are these pictures of what boys and girls really look like?"
"Yes," said Emily.
"No," said Sophie.
"Sometimes," said Jacob.
"I wonder," said Ms. Reeves, "if there is another way?
Everyone has to use the bathroom, right?"

"Maybe the signs should be pictures of toilets!" shouted Noah.
Everyone giggled.

"We should make our own bathroom signs," said Sophie.

"And rules," said Jacob. "Like, if you're in the bathroom and
you see a kid who doesn't look like you—leave them alone."

"Or 'I have to pee, so let me be!'" said Noah.
The giggling turned to cheers.
"Great ideas!" said Ms. Reeves. "Let's get to work!"

The afternoon was filled
with markers and laughter.

New bathroom signs went up.

The bunny signs were funny.

Jacob and Sophie stopped outside the bathroom doors.

"Do you think it's OK?" asked Jacob.
Sophie smiled. "I think it will be," she said.
And in they went.

## Authors' Note

**W**hen our son Sam was in kindergarten, he had waist-length blond hair and a gentle smile. His favorite outfit was a pink dress. Everyone who met him assumed he was a girl, and he didn't mind.

Sam's interests were a mix of traditional "girl" things like ballet, make-believe, and art, mixed with traditional "boy" things like knights, castles, and dinosaurs. Clinically, children like Sam are called gender-nonconforming; we liked to call him a pink boy—the male equivalent of a tomboy.

We didn't think there was anything wrong with being a pink boy, but we knew Sam was different—and different isn't always easy. In order to support Sam, we worked hard to educate his teachers about gender-nonconforming children. In turn, his teachers taught lessons about gender, difference, and acceptance. We were surprised how quickly and comfortably Sam's classmates took to looking at Sam—and the world—in a whole new way.

But the bathrooms at school were used by kids who weren't necessarily Sam's classmates. Older kids, bigger kids, kids who hadn't been taught these lessons looked at Sam—and didn't like what they saw. He was verbally and physically attacked by children who had not been taught to be kind in the face of unexpected difference.

It wasn't just school bathrooms that were a problem. It was restaurant bathrooms, and playground bathrooms, and airport bathrooms. It was the zoo bathroom where a little boy with a crew cut screamed, "Get out of here!" and tried to punch Sam—while Sam was using the urinal. There was no public bathroom our son could use without an adult along to guarantee his safety.

It doesn't have to be that way. Your home probably doesn't have a "men's bathroom" and a "women's bathroom." It just has a bathroom the whole family uses. As gender-nonconforming young people enter the mainstream, schools and institutions are starting to adjust to their presence and make changes. After all, everyone needs to use the bathroom. It's not a choice; it's a necessity. Wouldn't it be great if everybody could do it in safety?

*—Sarah and Ian Hoffman*